Imagine! Rhymes of Hope to Shout Together
This edition published in 2022 by Red Comet Press, LLC, Brooklyn, NY

Original title: *Magari! Rimi dei desideria da strillare insieme*
First published in Italy by Camelozampa in 2021
© 2021 Camelozampa
Original Italian text © 2021 Bruno Tognolini
Illustrations © 2021 Giulia Orecchia
English Translation © 2022 Red Comet Press
Translated by Denise Muir

Library of Congress Control Number: 2021946888
ISBN (HB): 978-1-63655-014-5
ISBN (Ebook): 978-1-63655-015-2

21 22 23 24 25 TLF 10 9 8 7 6 5 4 3 2 1

Manufactured in China

RED
COMET
PRESS RedCometPress.com

Bruno Tognolini

Giulia Orecchia

Imagine!

Rhymes of Hope to Shout Together

Translation by
Denise Muir

Red Comet Press • Brooklyn

If only my wish could be for each day
To gather all wishes in twinkling array
And grant them to everyone, stranger or kin
All of us chanting

Imagine!

If only rich uncles who knew how to fly
Would carry us presents across the sky
Buckets of coins stowed in the cabin
Gold by the gallon

Imagine!

If only the world outside could be taught
Not in the classroom—our teachers, they ought
To open the window, show how things happen
How much we'd fathom

Imagine!

If only tomorrow could be better than today
Tomorrow I'll be there, I'll help guide your way
If you don't know today, tomorrow you'll glean
And soon you'll be doing

Imagine!

If only my street or my whole neighborhood
Were a colorful garden or a bluebell wood
With trees tall enough to give rare birds an attic
No noisy traffic

Imagine!

If only what broke out in the Middle East
Instead of adult wars could be childlike peace
Give up the guns, all the bombs banished
By a bilingual chorus

If only the pirates, the vampires, the knights
That I see on TV or read of at night
Turned out to be real, shared a meal, cooked us salmon
We'd eat with abandon

Imagine!

If only I could wash right out of your head
The black thoughts that swirl like a cloud of dread
Push off the dark, make your days bright and golden
Bring back your smile

Imagine!

If only me and my animal friends
Could do a jaguar roar, join a singing bird band
Bleat like a billy goat, after a fashion
Shout it out loud, with a passion

Imagine!

If only my birthday would bring me this year
A bird to fly near me and chirp in my ear
"They got you a gift, but it won't be the last one
They filled a whole wagon"

Imagine!

If only you'd think of tomorrow today
Healing the planet and halting decay
Let birds nest in houses; no paving, no parking
Every day sparkling

Imagine!

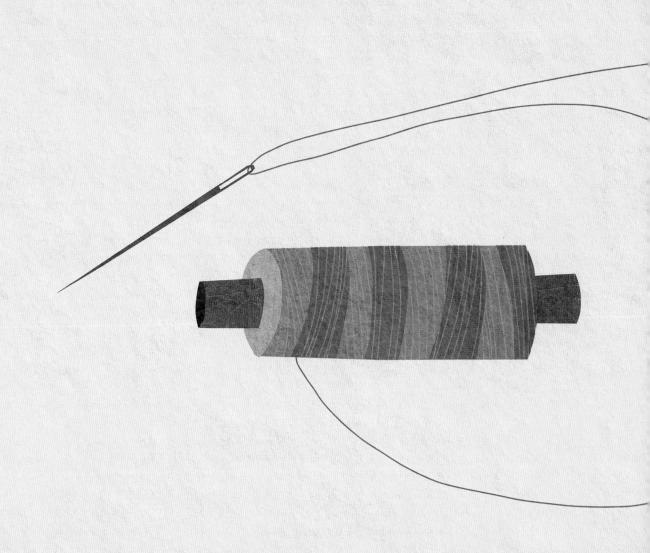

If only you'd tell me the reason you left
If only you'd see me, so sad and bereft
I'd give you my heart, you could sew it with satin
Our love to refasten

Imagine!

If only this family nest I call home
Could hold us forever, never to roam
My loved ones around me their days to share in
Together as one

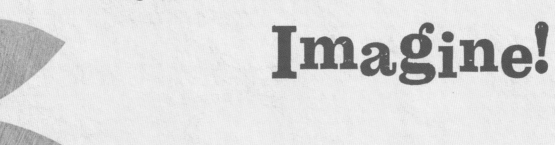

Imagine!

If only the borders in countries could end
A push and a shove to make governments repent
If we're all from nowhere, what'd be our reaction?
Maybe we'd learn to have more compassion

Imagine!

If only at lunchtime Grampy would bring
Some fried calamari and onion rings
From the place on the corner with the chef named Jasmine
Don't forget napkins.

Imagine!

If only me and my classmates, all equal at school
Could grow up remembering we'll forever be cool
No matter our hometown—the moon or Manhattan
No tolerating factions

Imagine!

If only Google could show me a map
Of where to find work for my darling dad
At home he just mopes, his face drawn and ashen
I wish he would play

Imagine!

If only one day that mean ugly creep
Who taunts me and haunts me, even in my sleep
Would wake up a donkey and bray in abandon
Hear how noisy he's gotten

Imagine!

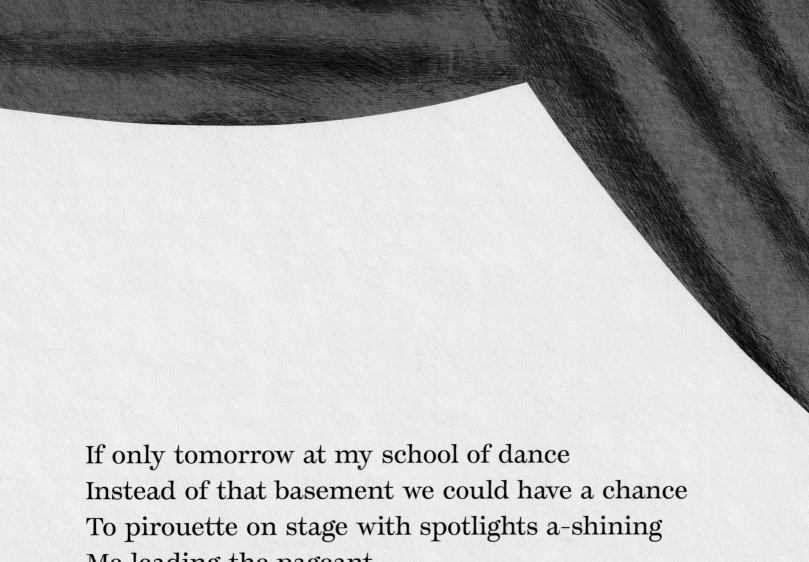

If only tomorrow at my school of dance
Instead of that basement we could have a chance
To pirouette on stage with spotlights a-shining
Me leading the pageant

Imagine!

If only tomorrow at the soccer game
For the penalty kicks coach calls my name
I shoot, get the goal, and all of a sudden
Cheers for me flood in

Imagine!

If only together all girls and boys
Could play soccer or dance, like sharing toys.
As equals on teams as on see-saws or swings
Everyone welcome

Imagine!

If only the officials who close our borders
Then hide the drownings to pretend all is in order
Could see the graves in the watery dungeon
Choose a kinder path

Imagine!

If only these things could change for the better
New days could dawn full of music and laughter,
A drum beat to make all our heartbeats align
With love all the time

Imagine!

If only a *new wish* could reach us each day
A light in our eyes that would come to stay
Shining each morning its magic so fine
Making us sing all of the time

Imagine!